Katie's Wish

Katie's Wish

Written and Illustrated by:

Susan Spierling Smith

Library of Congress Control Number:		2018903328
ISBN:	Hardcover	978-1-9845-1570-4
	Softcover	978-1-9845-1569-8
	eBook	978-1-9845-1568-1

Print information available on the last page.

Rev. date: 03/27/2018

To order additional copies of this book, contact:
Xlibris
1-888-795-4274
www.Xlibris.com
Orders@Xlibris.com
776588

Contents

1

A Long Ride Up North

Katie watched trees flashing by through the car window pelted by rain. She hugged her arms tight to her small body, still damp and cold inside the thin, light-blue jacket. Katie was hungry, but she didn't say anything. She still felt numb all over. Everything had happen so quickly. Katie couldn't believe that she was sitting in the back seat of this little, red hatchback car. She looked at the back of the driver's head, whose hair was blonde, almost yellow, and glowed like sun light.

The lady seemed nice, but Katie didn't know her. In fact, before two days ago, she had never even seen her.

Mama always told me not to talk to strangers, Katie thought, *Here I am trapped with this stranger and mama is not here to help me.*

Katie thought about her friends at school. She wondered if Torri would be playing with Tabatha now. Miss Hanes was teaching about Hawaii, and she was supposed to do the hula dance with both Torri and Tabatha at the diversity program in a couple of weeks. Now she wouldn't be there.

She thought about how proud Mama and Daddy were when she told them. Now for the first time, tears slid down her face. She tried not to think about them, but she saw Mama holding out her arms to her, and Daddy's big smile.

When he smiled, his eyes twinkled and he always winked at her.

Katie thought about how Miss Hanes was called to the office last week. When she came back, she had a strange look on her face with her eyes red and wet. She had called Katie out in the hall to talk to her. When they were in the hallway, Miss Hanes knelt down and wrapped her arms around Katie. She then looked at her and said softly, "Honey, something very bad has happened. There has been an accident. Your parents--they, they died." She then hugged Katie harder and started crying again.

Katie didn't cry. It wasn't true. It was April fool's day and Charles had already fooled her twice making her look at things that weren't there. Miss Hanes was just playing a very horrible joke on her. But Miss Hanes wasn't laughing, she was still crying and wiping at her tears that were streaming down her cheeks. She was hugging Katie so hard, that Katie could scarcely breathe. The principal came with Mrs. Brown, Katie's next door neighbor, and Mrs. Brown took her away from the school. The school that she had went to every since she started Kindergarten. Now she didn't know if she would ever see it or her friends again.

Even after Katie saw Mama and Daddy in the coffins, she still didn't cry. She just sat and stared. She heard everyone talking in hushed whispers as they gave her quick glances. Katie heard them say that she was to stay with kind Mrs. Brown. She didn't mind this as Mrs. Brown had been like a grandma to her. She didn't really have a grandma or grandpa.

She didn't have any aunts or uncles or cousins because her daddy had been an orphan and her mama was an only child whose parents died before Katie was born.

Then she heard the young lady who was now driving her away from everything, that Mrs. Brown was too old to care for a little girl for very long. Miss Karen, as the lady called herself, had said that she found out that Katie had an aunt. Katie was puzzled. Why didn't she know? Miss Karen said that it was her mother's older sister who lived Up North in a cabin in the woods.

So now Katie was on her way to stay with this aunt whom she had never heard of before. The car slowed and turned into a rest area. "Katie," Miss Karen turned to her. "Are you all right?"

Katie nodded and looked at all of the people getting out of their cars and walking through the blowing rain up the steep sidewalk to the big, brown public building on top of the hill.

"Come on Katie," Miss Karen urged, "get out and we will walk around and then you can use the restroom." Katie didn't move. "Look Katie, I know that this is hard for you, but your aunt seemed nice when I talked to her. I sent her a telegram and then she called me from a public phone. She must care to go to that bother," she paused searching for words and looked pleadingly at Katie, "and as long as she wants you, there is nothing I can do about it."

She looked as sad as Katie felt. "I don't know her," Katie whispered softly.

"I know Honey, but you will and she is your family." Miss Karen got out and opened the back door. She took Katie's hand. "Come on, lets walk. It'll be okay, you will see."

A couple of hours later they drove into a small town. A rustic gas station with two, antique red, pumps sat back away from the dirt road that was main street. An old gray building with a sign hanging crooked over the door with the words, 'General Store' in faded green paint sat right next to the muddy lane. There were a few other older buildings scattered here and there.

They pulled up next to an older model, brown, station wagon parked in front of the general store. A tall, thin, older lady in blue jeans and a brown, flannel shirt got out of the station wagon. Brown hair with steaks of gray was pulled back into a tight ponytail. Her face was long and thin and her green eyes were hard and cold.

She doesn't look anything like Mama, thought Katie, except her eyes are the same color, but Mama's were soft and gentle and smiling.

"What took you so long?" the aunt glared at both of them.

"I'm sorry you had to wait, but the traffic was bad. It was raining down state." Miss Karen explained. "This is Katie."

"Puny like your ma, ain't ya!" she thundered, "Well, come on. We ain't got all day."

Miss Karen transferred Katie's belongings into the mud covered station wagon. She handed the sack of stuffed animals and toys to Katie who had climbed into the car. Miss Karen leaned over and hugged Katie as she slipped her business card into her hand.

"Call me if you need anything, anything!" she said softly. She turned and walked quickly back to her car and drove away.

2

The Cabin in The Woods

The old station wagon was now creeping up a narrow, winding, muddy and sometimes rocky road. Water from the rain and snow that had melted from the spring sun, covered the entire roadway in places. Large trees crowded in on either side of the rutty track with their branches looming out over the car like giant hands. Katie held the sack of stuffed animals close to her, as her dark eyes peered out at the shadows.

"By the way," the old aunt snarled, "You won't be needing that number there on that card. You can't call that do-good social worker. I don't have a phone!" It was the first time she smiled but her eyes were still cold. Katie closed her eyes and pretended to be asleep.

When finally they pulled up to a little log cabin, her aunt told her to get out of the car. Katie looked around. The cabin had a porch running all across the front, with stacks of wood piled in neat rows next to it. The trees came right up close to the cabin and beautiful wild flowers were growing in clumps everywhere. Except for the road, which was more like a muddy trail and the cabin, it looked as if they were in the middle of a huge forest with no signs of people. Katie turned to pick up the sack of her favorite toys. Her aunt grabbed them from her.

"You won't be needing these!" In fact, you won't need any of this stuff, except maybe some clothes. My house is too small to be cluttered up with nonsense toys. Besides, you won't have time to play, The aunt threw her precious things back into the car.

"You need to get into the house. I'll show you how to do everything." Her aunt gave her a shove toward the house. "I bet your mother never taught you anything!"

"You can call me Aunt, she continued, "my name is Clara, but you don't know me good enough to call me by my name." When Katie didn't answer, the middle aged woman gave her a shove again.

"You hear me girl?" She demanded.

Katie managed a small, "Yes, Aunt." She bit her bottom lip to stop it from trembling.

"Fine, You do as I say and you'll be okay. First, I don't want to hear anything about your mother and her good-for-nothing husband. It is just as well that they are dead. She's been dead to me for a long time anyway. Too bad they had you though. At first, I said I wouldn't take you in, but then I got to thinking, maybe it wouldn't be a bad idea to have an extra pair of hands around here. I'm getting older and things are getting harder for me to do--like carrying water up the hill from the stream. That's right! I ain't got no electric up here. I gotta do everything and it ain't been easy lately. I wasn't expecting you to be so puny, though. You better be able to do more than you look like you can, else I'll send you packing. Then where will you go?" The aunt looked amused.

"That's right, you got nowhere to go but here, right? Ha!"She opened the door and pushed Katie into the one room cabin. She then walked over to the big, wood burning stove. Suddenly the aunt yelled, "Well, don't just stand there, get over here so I can show you how to do this stove! Then you can cook us some supper."

That was Katie's first day with her aunt from Up North. From there it got worse. Each day, Katie had to get up before the sun and build a fire in the wood cook stove. She had to carry in more wood from outside, and then begin breakfast. The only thing her mother had let her do was make toast and warm things in the microwave oven. She had told her that a nine year old was too little to cook. Now two months after she came to live with her aunt, she could fry ham, bacon, potatoes and hamburgers. She could make scrambled eggs, pancakes, biscuits and coffee. She had to learn fast, because each time she made a mistake, her aunt would cuff her on the head.

3

Smoke in The Cabin

At first, no matter how hard Katie tried, she couldn't do anything right and she suffered the consequences. The first time she built a fire in the woodstove, she almost smoked them out for a week. It took her forever to light the chunks of wood--in fact, at first it was impossible. Her aunt woke up to the noise she was making and yelled at her. Old aunt then laughed at her when she watched her try to light the big pieces of wood.

"Don't believe you have anthing between your ears!" She said as she grabbed the matches! Here, use the kindling in the wood box. And grab some old newspaper over there." Katie quickly snatched some paper and wadded it up as her aunt showed her. "Here, see. Light the paper and then put the kindling on it. And don't forget to open the draft." With that the aunt hurried outside to do some chores.

Katie looked around fror the draft. She had no idea what it was, but she was afraid to go out and ask her aunt. *Maybe it is the window she thought.* She opened the window only a crack because it was still chilly out. The kindling had started to burn so she added a couple of bigger sticks of wood on top of the little fire soon the wood was blazing. She felt so proud of herself and was about to go tell her aunt, when suddenly thick grayish black smoke started seeping out of the top of the stove.

At first, it came slowly and then in huge puffs until the entire cabin was full of the wispy stuff. Katie's eyes burned and she coughed as the smoke stung her throat. She opened the door and ran smack into her aunt's strong arms.

"YOU STUPID CHILD! Can't you do anything right! Now look at what you did. You probably ruined everything in the cabin." The aunt grabbed both of her forearms and started shaking her. She then let go of Katie and slapped her hard across the face. Aunt shoved her aside, opened the damper (a key-looking thing sticking out of the pipe going up to the of chimney), and set about opening all of the windows and the door. She made Katie wash everything in the cabin.

The next day Katie had to wash all of the bedding, curtains and clothes that were in the house. She had to wash them in a big tub with a scrub board which was a piece of metal that looked like it had been folded and like an accordion. Her hands hurt from the yellowish hard lye soap and several times she scraped her fingers on the rough metal of the scrub board.

Several days later, Katie was making vegetable soup, which was one of the first things she learned to cook. Her aunt said that any fool could throw a soup together and cook it, so she should be good at it. She finished cutting up the carrots, potatoes and onions and put them in the boiling water with a ham bone that she had simmered for an hour.

She heard a bang against the window and looked up to see a tiny squirrel looking in at her. She laughed, grabbed a piece of bread and ran out of the house. When outside she stopped and walked slowly around the corner toward the window. The squirrel was still there looking inside. She made soft clucking sounds to the squirrel. It turned and looked at her. She talked in a low, soft gentle voice to it, coaxing it forward with the bread.

After several minutes, she was able to get it to come as close as her feet. She dropped the bread and watched the squirrel pick it up. Slowly she squatted down so she could watch closer. She was fascinated by the way the squirrel used his feet like hands, turning the bread as he ate.

Katie stood up and noticed the blossoms on the little bush by the window. They were covered with beautiful orange and black butterflies. There were too many to count. She tried to touch one, but it flew away. Katie laughed out loud at the beauty of the little winged creatures. They looked to her like flowers floating in the air. She ran around chasing them as they darted about. Then a horrible scorching smell came through the opened door.

"Oh, no!" Katie hollered, "The soup!" She tore back into the smoke-filled house. A black cloud was swirling up toward the ceiling from the big pan on the stove. "Oh Great!" Katie moaned, "I forgot to put enough water in the pan!"

She grabbed a dishtowel, wrapped it around the handle of the pan and carried it outside and sat it on the porch. Katie hurried around opening all of the windows and madly fanned the air with the towel. She poured water and lye soap into the charred pan and let it set. Then she went back into the house to see what else she could fix for lunch. To her dismay, there wasn't anything else left that she knew how to cook. She finally found a jar of peanut butter and made sandwiches.

By the time her aunt came home from the woods, she had scraped and cleaned the pan so that there was only a little bit of tell tale brown on the inside. To her relief the smoke was gone from the house, but her aunt knew something wasn't right.

"What's that funny smell?" she asked. Then she went to the stove. "Where's the soup I told you to make? I saw that hambone out beside the house. You gave it to those stupid animals didn't you?" She then noticed the peanut butter sandwiches on the table.

"What? What? Do you think I want peanut butter sandwiches after I worked hard cutting trees all day? Okay! I'll eat the sandwiches and you can go to bed. You don't deserve any food until you can learn to do your job right!"

So Katie again went to bed without any supper. This was her aunt's favorite punishment. She would send Katie to bed earlier than she ever had to go before and she refused to feed her the last meal of the day.

4

Weeding The Garden

It was only a few days after this incident, when Katie's aunt decided it was time for Katie to weed the garden. Katie was raised in the city and had never seen vegetable plants before. She was trying hard to concentrate on the plants, while her aunt showed them to her, but they all looked so similar. Her aunt's voice faded away in a raspy drone, as Katie stared off into the woods. She wondered how far the trees went and what other kinds of animals lived beyond the area she had explored on her trips to the creek. Her aunt's sudden harsh voice startled her.

"Are you listening to me or are you daydreaming again? Now I want you to pull all the weeds you can get up in two hours." She handed Katie a heavy hoe that was twice as tall as she was. "Well, get busy! I'm going down yonder to check on the wild strawberries. If they are ripe, I should get a bucket full." Her aunt grabbed a small, plastic, peanut butter pail and hurried off down the trail to the woods.

Dismayed, Katie turned to stare at the wide garden with fifty feet rolls of foliage. Each roll was packed with different kinds of plants all mixed together. Katie couldn't remember which was vegetables and which was the dreaded weeds. She tried to maneuver the awkward long handle of the hoe, but it was so heavy she couldn't get it to dig into the ground. She gave up and began pulling the plants by hand. Katie decided that the vegetable, maybe it was carrots, would probably have the largest leaves, so she began to pull all of the tiny ones in the middle. She bent over her task with determination. Soon sweat was rolling down her face. She wiped the tickling wetness away with a dirt covered hand leaving muddy streaks across her face. Her mouth was dry and her throat ached for water, but she was afraid if she stopped and went into the house, her aunt would come back and catch her not working.

She had two whole rows weeded when her aunt walked up with a bucket of little red berries. Katie stood up, smiling, proud that she had done so much before Aunt returned. The old woman put the berry pail down on the porch and walked over to Katie.

"You stupid, brat!" a red faced Aunt roared. "How could you be so ignorant! How could anyone not know the difference between a carrot and a pig weed?" She was shaking her fists in the air. "Now I have to replant the whole two rows and we will have to wait that much longer to have carrots for stew!"

Katie slowly backed away from her ranting aunt. "Hey! Where do you think your going? Get back here! You are going to stay out here and pull every single pig weed if it takes you all night! Maybe by the time you are finished you will know the difference."

Katie dropped down on her knees by the row of pigweeds. She was still thirsty, but she didn't dare say anything. She bent her head toward the ground so that her aunt couldn't see the tears that ran down her mud, streaked face.

I wish just once I could please her and not do everything wrong, Katie thought. Then she had an idea. She would learn to cook so good that her aunt would have to notice. She had found an old cookbook that had her grandmother's name on it. She would study it and find out all of the secrets about cooking.

5

Soap Making

Several weeks went by with Katie busy every day doing chores. However, every chance she got she would read her grandmother's cookbook, jotting down notes to study later. She hid it under her pillow and only looked at it when her aunt went outside. Every day she would learn about a new recipe. She tried to stick with basic foods so her aunt wouldn't realize what she was doing and take the cookbook away from her. She managed to make everything she cooked taste extra good. Her aunt didn't say anything, but she did eat more and she didn't criticize her cooking any longer.

One day when she thought the aunt was out in the woods, Katie was intent on a new recipe for meatloaf. First she coped the recipe down and then she would try to memorize it so she could make it without referring to the cookbook or notes. Suddenly she heard her aunt on the steps of the porch. She scrambled to shove the book under the pillow before her aunt walked in.

"Since you're getting a mite better with your cooking." the aunt bellowed out as she swung the door open, "I think it is high time you learn how to make lye soap."

"Yes Aunt," Katie said as she hurried away from her bed.

"This is the best time for making lye!" She beamed. It was still wet outside even though the sun was shinning brightly. It had rained for several hours and the air felt damp. Her aunt led her over to the big wooden barrel that stood beside the corner of the house under the eaves drop. It had collected all the water that poured off the roof and now was brimming over.

"First we gotta get this water here," Aunt dipped a ten-gallon pail in the barrel and pulled it out full of water. "Rain water makes the soap softer," she handed the pail of water to Katie. Katie almost fell under the weight of the full bucket, but shifted her weight. She regained her balance and put all of her might into carrying the heavy load to the other wooden barrel forty feet on the other side of the yard. She was determined not to fail again.

Aunt took the heavy pail from her and set it beside the second wooden barrel, which was sitting on bricks to lift it off from the ground. The barrel had a hole drilled in the bottom of it with a plug stuck in it. There were several bricks inside of the barrel. Her aunt had put a board over them and then placed some straw on top of the board. "That's so the hole won't get plugged up from the ashes," she explained.

"What ashes?" Katie looked into the empty barrel.

"The ashes over there," her aunt pointed to a pile of gray stuff, which had a thin stream of smoke curling out of it. "I want you to go get that other tin pail and fill it with the warm ashes. I burned that this morning from the hardwood." Katie carried pail after pail of the sticky, hot ashes. Each time she brought a pail to her aunt, she would dump it into the large barrel and firmly pack it down. When finally the barrel was full, her aunt made an opening in the center of the ashes, and poured the water that Katie had carried earlier.

"There now, go get more water," Her aunt handed the pail to Katie. She carried two more pails before her aunt was satisfied. Katie's shoulders began to ache.

"That will do," her aunt covered the barrel with the wooden head and then raised it at the back so that the liquid would run toward the front. "Tomorrow you can add more water."

Three weeks later, her aunt removed the plug and drew off the lye into the wooden pail. "Here," she smiled, "this liquid is strong enough to float an egg, and that means it's strong enough to make soap."

"I thought that was what we already did," said Katie. "How do you make soap?" She was fascinated. She didn't know anybody that had ever made soap before. In fact, she didn't even know people could make soap at home. She had noticed that her aunt's soap looked different than the soap her mama bought at the store.

"I didn't expect you to know how. That's why I'm teaching you so next time you can do it by yourself while I'm out in the woods. Come here, do as I say and you might learn how. First you gotta melt the lard. In the old days, we rendered beef fat to make tallow, but I don't butcher no more. I'm getting too old to handle raising cows." Her aunt fetched a big, black, iron kettle from behind the cabin. She made a fire outside and hung the pan over the blaze from a tall tripod. She then put several pounds of lard into the kettle. She stirred the lard a long time until it melted. She took the kettle off the tripod with a large hook and let the lard cool.

"Ok, now go get me the lye and put it in the lard." she ordered. Katie ran for the lye, which had cooled, she poured some into a pail. In her hurry, she spilled some of the lye on her hand. It burned as if it were on fire. She held back the tears and ran to her aunt with the remaining lye. She tried to pour it into the pan slowly like her aunt had told her, but her hand burned so badly that she dumped it in. Suddenly the fumes shot up and the mixture began splattering everywhere. Some of the hot acidic liquid hit her aunt's arm. Her aunt yelled out swearing at Katie. "You are the dumbest kid I ever saw!" Then she noticed Katie's hand.

"What on earth did you do to your hand? Don't tell me you dipped your hand in lye. Oh my goodness, child, come on. We gotta get some vinegar on that and my arm, too."

Her aunt looked worried. She hurried into the house with Katie and doctored them both up with cold water and vinegar. "I guess I'll have to finish it alone and wait to have you help until next year," she continue, "but you can watch now so you will know how to make it yourself later."

Katie's hand hurt so badly that she wanted to cry but bit her lip and watched her aunt finish the job of making soap. When it was all done, her aunt had her wrap the bars in paper. Katie almost felt as if her aunt could be kind. She had relished her aunt's touch when the older lady washed her hand. *If only she could always be like that,* but then she shook her thoughts away. It wouldn't do any good to wish. Tomorrow her aunt will still treat her the same.

6

Katie's Wish

This morning there was still a chill in the air even though it was almost July. Her aunt was pleased with the breakfast because she didn't criticize it. She just grunted her approval and began shaving the food into her mouth.

"I want you to get water this morning and after that, I'll show you how to chop the wood," she said between mouthfuls.

After Katie cleared the table and washed the dishes, she picked up the tin, five-gallon water pail that was sitting by the door and walked out into the bright sunlight. Her aunt was hooking an old trailer up to her rundown tractor.

"Now don't dillydally," she snapped. "I'm going to get us some more wood and I want you to chop it when I get back."

Her aunt's tractor disappeared down the rutty, two, track trail. As the putting sound drifting farther and farther into the woods, Katie filled her lungs with the sweet, crisp air. She looked around smiling. She loved the forest and all of the green plants and pretty wild flowers splattered around the ground. Katie stooped down and picked a yellow lily growing by the porch. A squirrel poked his head out from under the porch steps.

"Come on, little fellow," Katie coaxed. She had hoped she would see him this morning. She took a piece of pancake that she had saved from breakfast out of her pocket. She had almost tamed him enough to get close enough to touch him. She tossed him the food. He ran up and sat on two legs, with the other two feet, he picked up the offering and began nibbling it. Katie laughed out loud. She then picked up the pail and hurried down the steep trail to the creek.

Today all of her friends were about. The birds followed Katie and seemed to sing just to her. The chipmunks ran along beside her. She laughed as they darted in and out running around her., This was her favorite thing to do. She loved the freedom of running through the woods and pretending that she could stay all day. It made all of the hard work and harsh words go away for a short time.

Katie reached the lapping water and lay down on the big, moss-covered rock that jutted out over the bank. She could look directly down into the water. She loved gazing at the fish that swam so near she could almost touch them. One very large fish seemed to understand her feelings. It was weird, but he was always there when she came and didn't leave until she did.

Katie had started talking to him a few weeks ago, when she first noticed him. She had told him how she missed her mother and father, her teacher, and her friends. Katie told the fish how mean her aunt was to her. She sadly told him how she wouldn't be able to finish the third grade because she didn't need school now. Aunt said since only the social worker, who was miles away on the other side of the state, knew she was there, no one would know if her aunt sent her to school or not. Her aunt had said that the school was too far away. Katie told the fish how she had to work hard from morning until dark, without ever having time to play. It was easy to share the hurtful things with fish. It made her feel a little better each time. It made her think of fish as her best friend.

Today she knew she couldn't stay long so she had raced all the way in order to give her more time to talk. She had paid little attention to the swinging pail that had banged against her leg the whole way, except to fling it on the bank as soon as the path opened up to the creek.

Now as she leaned toward the water, she spotted the fish. He swam up so that he was right under her head. He glanced up at her with understanding eyes. She suddenly became very sad when she saw his kind face. A big tear rolled down her face into the water on top of the fish.

"Oh! I do wish I could be a fish. Yes! I wish--I wish I could be a fish. Then I could swim away and be free," she said in distress.

"Okay! If that is what you want."

Katie jerked her head up and looked around, "Who said that?" she asked in a hushed voice.

"I did. Down here." The fish poked his nose above the water.

Katie looked down and shook her head, "But you are a fish! You can't talk!"

"Well, I usually don't talk, but this isn't a usual case. I've been listening to you for weeks, but you never cried before. I can't stand to seen anyone cry, especially a pretty, little girl. I can turn you into a fish for a short while, but I really can't solve your problem. However, I think I know someone who can," Fish finally stopped.

"Who?" Katie asked, "Who will help me?"

"Old King Crab. He can, but you never know about him. It depends on his mood, but it is worth a try. It is a long way and you might get tired. Do you still want to try?" fish asked.

"Oh yes! I'd do anything to get away from Aunt", Katie said.

"Okay then," Fish said as he spun in a circle, "you are a fish!"

7

Danger In The Lake

Suddenly Katie was in the water. Her arms and legs were gone; in there place were a tail and fins. She spun around, swam deep into the water and then shot back up to the surface to the fish.

"Oh!" she gasp, "This is great! Look how fast I can swim!"

"Okay, okay," fish said, trying to hide a smile, "but you need to save your strength. We have a long way to go. Come on, follow me."

They swam down the long creek, weaving in and out of the obstacles of branches, rocks, and sometimes garbage that cropped up in the way. They passed other fish, but most were smaller than them and quickly darted out of their way. Several of them waved or nodded their heads as they glided away.

"You don't have to worry much about the other fish here. They are all my friends. They call me Carp. That is my name so you can call me Carp, too." He continued, "It is when we get to the big lake that we have to be careful."

Soon the river opened up into a great body of water.

"This is it! This is the Big Lake."

"Keep your eyes opened!" Carp warned.

They swam for some time when said, "Oh, oh! Watch out! Do you see that big shadow up there?" He pointed with his fin.

"What is it?" Katie asked, swimming quickly over to the nervous fish.

"It is a swimming fisherman with a nasty spear gun. We have to move quickly away from him, because if he sees us, we don't have much of a chance to get away from that spear. If we dart back and forth, it will make it harder for him to hit us," Carp explained.

"Oh! Let's go!" He is turning, the fish abruptly dashed away. Just then the shadow turned toward them.

"COME ON! COME ON!" Carp yelled. Katie sped after him with a sudden spurt of energy. She heard something whiz past her ear.

"Hurry, Katie! That was the spear! He has to reload so if we keep going, we will lose him," Carp encouraged her.

After a few more minutes, Carp said, "There! We can slow down. How are you doing?"

"I'm tired and scared, but I guess I'm okay", she answered.

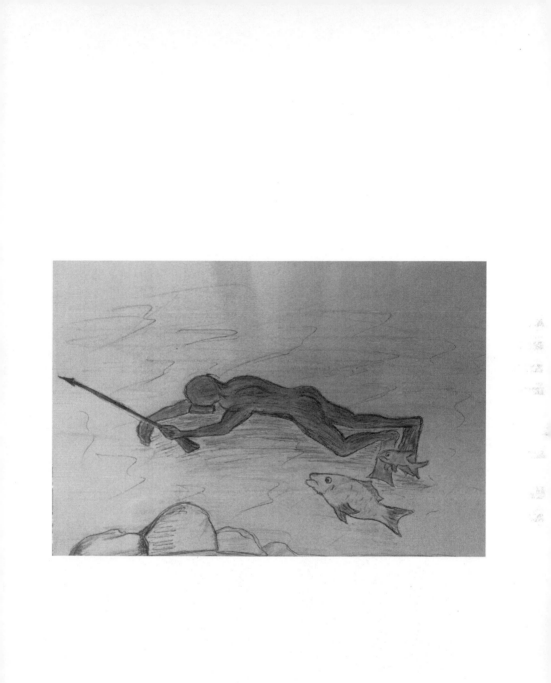

8

Tangled in Garbage

They swam on a while longer and Katie relaxed enough to look around. She noticed the rocks on the bottom of the clear water. It was all so different and wonderful looking from under the lake, just like the shows she saw with her parents on television. Suddenly she noticed a shiny object just a few feet from her. She swam quickly to it and poked at it with her nose. It popped loose and to her disappointment, it was just the top of a pop can. Then she noticed other garbage scattered around, some half covered by the sand and some stuck in the rocks. She was disgusted at the thoughtlessness of whoever dumped this stuff in the great lake.

She turned to call her friend, "Carp! Come over here and look at this mess! Carp! Carp! Where are you?" She swam around looking desperately for the kind fish. "Please, Carp! You have to answer me."

She began to panic when she realized that he had swum on without knowing that she had stopped. *I can't believe I did that again. Every time I start thinking to myself, something bad happens. I have to find Carp,* she began talking to herself, *I don't have any idea where I am at or how to get out of the lake. In fact, I don't even know how to turn back into a girl. What if I'm down here when I turn back! I don't even know how to swim that good. Oh, what am I going to do?*

Abruptly her body was jerked to a stop. She turned and twisted, but her body was stuck fast to a rock. She could finally manage to bend enough so that she could see what was holding her. It was a piece of plastic that must have held bottles together at one time. One end was stuck firmly between two rocks and she had somehow swum through the loop that stuck out with realizing it.

I'm going to die here! she thought, *At least I will be able to see Mommy and Daddy again.* She closed her eyes and waited to drift off into, well she really didn't know what. Katie was jolted out of her thoughts by something or someone tugging on her side.

"Who are you and what are you doing to me?" She tried to pull away, but couldn't move.

"Don't be afraid. I'm trying to help you." A deep voice boomed. "How in the world did you get yourself into this fix? Here, here, hold still, can't you?"

"Sorry, but you frighten me!" Katie's heart was beating fast and her body shaking.

"Calm down! Its going to be okay. Just give me a moment or two," the voice went on. "Where did you come from? I have never seen you in these parts before. By the way, my name is Captain. They call me that because I like to explore old ship wrecks. There are a lot of them, too, cause the waters over head are unpredictable." He began sawing at the plastic around her body with his long, sharp nose.

"I'm Katie. I just came here with my friend Carp, only I lost him. I was trying to find him when I got caught in this thing. There should be a law against making anything that could harm anyone."

"Well, you know people. They don't think about any one but themselves! Never did think much of them. You gotta watch out for them all the time. They tear around on top with those loud, fast contraptions. Gotta be careful not to get to close up there, cause you never know when one of em will whiz past." He continued to nod his head back and forth as he tried to tear the synthetic trap away from her middle. After an agonizing few moments, it ripped loose and she broke free.

Katie turned to thank her rescuer. "Oh!" Katie said surprised. "You are a sword fish! But this is fresh water. My teacher told us last fall that ocean fish couldn't live in fresh water. Why are you in a fresh water lake?"

"Well, that's a long story, but to make it short, I escaped from a ship overhead. They caught me off the coast of the Atlantic Sea. Ah, how I miss that salty paradise. Anyway, they had me in a big tank and was taking me to some fate I didn't know about and wasn't about to find out. I busted a hole in that thin glass and flipped overboard. And that is the long and short of it. I've been here every since. It's not bad here, but a little too tame for me. Not salty enough either. Though I guess I can live in fresh water cause I'm here and I ain't dead"

"What an exciting story. You must miss your family and friends though." Katie though about how much she missed her parents and her friends at school.

"Oh that I do, but can't do much about that. I made lots of friends here, though, some real good friends. In fact, your friend, Carp, he's one of them. I just saw him swim by 'fore I saw you. He's not that far ahead of you. I'll take you to him."

"That won't be necessary, Captain," Carp swam up to them. "Much obliged to you. I saw you swim by and turned to tell Katie who you were and I didn't see her. I swam all over looking before I followed you here. I was going to ask for your help, but I see you already gave it to us. We would love to stay and talk, but we have to go now. We are in a big hurry." He told his old friend all about Katie's plight.

"I wish I could go with you but I also have urgent business in the opposite direction. I wish you Godspeed. Goodbye, hope to see you again soon. Good luck Katie. Sorry about what I said about people. Didn't mean you."

Carp checked Katie where the plastic had dug into her. "Well, it might be a little sore for a while, but the skin is okay. Nothing is really damaged. How do you feel? You okay?"

Katie nodded. "Yes, I'm fine."

"Okay, let's get going. It's not much further, Now we have to swim deep. King Crab is usually on his throne on the bottom," Carp said as he headed down. Katie dove after him.

The biggest fish Katie had ever seen soon stopped them. "Halt! Who goes there?" The huge creature bellowed at them.

"Who is he?" Katie whispered to Carp.

"That is Sturgeon, the King Crab's guard."

"It's me, Carp," he answered the giant, guard fish. "I need to see the King. I have a friend who needs his help. What kind of mood is he in?"

"Oh, hi Carp, I didn't recognize you with your friend. Well, you know the King. He is pretty crabby today. I don't know if you even want to talk to him." Sturgeon shook his head.

"Well, we don't have much choice. Katie only has a while left before she changes back to a little girl and we still have to travel back to the creek. Just tell him that we are here."

"Okay, wait here," Sturgeon disappeared into the murky water near the bottom. Soon he was back.

"You are lucky. He will see you, but I don't know if it will do you any good. He's pretty short with everyone today," Sturgeon turned and swam away. "Come on, follow me," he called back.

"I can't see anything!" Katie cried.

"Just grab my tail and don't worry, it will clear up in a minute," Carp said. The water did clear up and there in front of them sat a very small King crab on a tall chair. Katie thought the chair looked a little like the chairs that the life guards used on the beach that her mama used to take her to.

9

Three Magic Pebbles

King Crab looked up annoyed, "Yeah, Yeah, so what do you want? Come on, I don't have all day!"

"Thank you for seeing us, Sir," Carp said smoothly. "I know how busy you are, but I have a very important problem"."

"Everybody has problems!" the King interrupted, "so what's your big problem?"

"This is Katie, Your Majesty, and the problem is hers. I was only able to get her here, but I can't help her situation, only you can do that."

"Yes, yes! I do have the most power," the King said softening a little bit. "Well, little fish, what's wrong?"

"Well, first of all I'm not a fish. I'm a little girl." Katie then told King Crab everything about what had happened to her starting with how her wonderful parents were killed and ending with the plight of her cruel aunt.

"Oh my, now that's a story!" the tiny crab said as he wiped a tear from his huge eye. "Ump", He cleared his throat, "now, ah, now well, let me see." His voice became gruff again. "I can help you, but you must follow my directions. Can you do that?"

King peered at her with one eye opened. "I'm going to give you a jar with three magic pebbles in it. Each morning when you fix your aunt's coffee, you must put one pebble in her cup. It will instantly dissolve in the hot liquid. Do this for three days. Each day that you put a magic pebble into the coffee and she drinks it, she will become kinder and remember what it was like to be a little girl. Maybe you can even help her understand why she is so mean. Can you do that?" He leaned forward and offered her the jar with the precious stones.

"Oh, I don't know what to say. Thank you! You are very kind," Katie said as she swam up and took the miniature jar."

"It's nothing! Now go on, I don't have anymore time for you," King Crab said gruffly as he waved them away.

"Thank you, Sir," Carp said, "You are as wise and generous as everyone says."

"Bah! What are you trying to do? Ruin my reputation? Now get out of here!" King commanded.

Carp and Katie turned and swam quickly away before the King changed his mind about the magic. Sturgeon accompanied them for a short while until they were through the murky water.

He stopped when the muddiness cleared and said, "Good luck, Katie. I wish you well. I can't go any further. There are fishermen with spears that have been after me for years. I am quite a legend around here for being the largest fish in these waters. I must be careful."

"We know about the spears," Katie nodded, "Thank you for all of your help and may you have a long and happy life."

"Thank you, and the same to you," Sturgeon turned to his friend, "Goodbye, Carp. You don't get out here much. It was good to see you again. Take care of Katie." He then turned and disappeared into the greenish-grey, murky water.

We don't have much time left, we have to hurry," Carp said to Katie as they swam off. There was no sign of the fisherman as they swam out of the big lake up into the small creek. They were halfway up the creek when Katie's energy ran out. She tried to go on, but she was so tired she couldn't breathe well. She finally just stopped.

Carp turned to see Katie hanging on to a branch. "What's the matter, Katie?" Her friend cried in alarm. "We have to keep going!"

"I--I can't! I'm tired. I--can't go any farther." Katie gasped.

"You have to Katie," Carp encouraged. "It's almost time for you to turn back into a girl. I'm afraid you will drown if we don't hurry."

"But, I can't. I'm just too tired." Katie closed her eyes.

"Hey!" Carp said loudly, "I know, here, let me pull you. Just hang on. Can you do that?"

She clung onto him as he darted in and around the branches, rocks and logs. An under current began rapidly pulling a Katie and she could no longer hold onto Carp. Suddenly she was swiftly spinning around and around. Everything whirled around her. She could no longer see Carp.

10

Just A Dream?

"Carp! Carp!" Katie was trying to yell, but her voice was just a whisper. She struggled to open her eyes. She squinted at her surroundings. She was laying on the moss-covered rock. The sun was beating down on her and she was very dry.

"Oh, no!' Katie moaned out loud. "I fell asleep. It was just a dream! Now I'm late and Aunt will beat me!" She grabbed the tossed water pail and quickly filled it with the cool stream water. She hurried as fast as she could with the heavy pail splashing water in every direction. She stumbled up the narrow path, tripping now and again over roots and twigs. She didn't notice the birds and chipmunks chasing beside her in a silent game of follow the leader. Water from the pail continued to slop out as her ran.

When she came in view of the cabin, she saw her aunt driving up the bumpy, dirt road on the old, screeching tracker. She had only manage to get to the porch with the half empty pail of water, before her aunt had jumped off the tractor and was beside her.

"You lazy little whelp! You were playing with those animals in the woods again and look! You spilled the water. It's not even half full," her aunt was red faced.

She grabbed Katie by the ear and pulled her to the woodpile. "Here, get that ax and give it to me," old aunt pointed at a large ax stuck in a stomp. Katie pried it loose after some effort and handed it to her aunt.

"Watch me! This is the way you chop wood. I know you probably thought that it comes chopped, but I split that wood over there last summer." She showed Katie how to hold an ax and swing it so that the ax head would do most of the work. Then she left to unload the wood from the trailer.

Katie worked hard, but couldn't seem to make the ax work like her aunt did. It kept bouncing off the block of wood or it would get stuck and she couldn't pull it free without tremendous effort. Sweat was dripping from her face and still she hadn't managed to chop one block of wood.

Her aunt came over and watched her. She snatched the ax and pushed Katie as she hollered, "Go on, you useless thing! Get in the house and cook dinner, but don't eat anything. You are going to scrub the cabin floor and then go to bed without eating. Maybe then you will learn to be responsible and do what I tell you to do."

Katie turned and ran into the house. She fixed her aunt's meal and then scrubbed the wooden floor. Tears dropped from her face into the mop pail as she rung out the rag mop. *It is worse than before*, she thought, *all I can do is dream stupid dreams and they don't change anything.*

Her aunt came in with muddy shoes and dirty hands. She walked across the clean floor to the little stand with a pan of water and a brown bar of soap. She began washing her hands as she glanced at the food on the table waiting for her. She then looked critically at the floor. Katie held her breathe as she continued to wash the pots and pans.

"At least you can half way cook and scrub, but don't think that is going to get you off the hook that easy. Tomorrow you are still going to learn to chop wood or wish you had. Now get to bed!"

Katie started to get ready for bed. "What are you doing!" the old aunt roared, "You don't need pajamas! Maybe you'll learn more if you sleep in your work clothes. Just get to bed!"

Katie hurried to her small bed at the far corner of the big room. Her aunt's bed was on the other side of the one room cabin, so at least at night, she could have a little space from her. She closed her eyes, and though she was hungry, Katie immediately fell to sleep.

11

A Nice Surprise

Katie woke up before the sun rose, even before the ticking alarm clock rang. She reached down and felt something hard in her pocket. She pulled it out and slipped out of bed. She put it down on the table by the lantern. She lit the kerosene lamp and picked the object up. She looked at it closely and gasped. It was a small jar with three little pebbles inside.

Katie's heart began to race. *Could it be?* She quickly shoved it back into her pocket. She turned to see her aunt hugging the blankets in her sleep as she snored softly.

Katie began to start the fire in the wood, cooking stove. As soon as the wood was crackling red, and ashes had formed, she put the coffee pot on the iron burner. Shortly she had pancake batter ready to go on the stove and the bacon was sizzle ling in the frying pan. Katie dropped the batter on to a hot griddle and soon had two stacks of steaming pancakes ready for the table. She set the table with plates and silver ware. Next she put the butter and maple syrup next to the plates.

The aroma from the coffee was strong and sweet and penetrated deep into the aunt's sleep. Her aunt began to stir and then sat up. She rubbed her head and got out of bed. She slowly picked up her clothes and walked out to the out door bathroom called the out house. By the time she came back and washed up, Katie had the food on the table and was pouring her aunt's coffee by the stove.

Katie slowly reached into her pocket and pulled out the little jar. She took one stone out and slipped it in the cup of coffee. Katie looked to check if her aunt was watching, but she was pulling her hair back into a tight ponytail. Katie quickly stirred the coffee and was surprised to notice that the stone disappeared. It had melted faster than a lump of sugar.

"Well," her aunt was saying, "I guess it did you good to be punished last night. This is nice to wake up to. But remember, you are still going to chop all of the wood starting today." Aunt sat down and stabbed the pancakes. She then set to work making them disappear. After she had finished wolfing down the food she reached for her coffee.

"What's wrong? You're not eating. Go on, set down and eat. You gotta build that scrawny body up so you can really work!' She sipped her coffee slowly with a slow smile forming on her face.

Katie sat down and stabbed a pancake. Even though she was hungry, she was so anxious about the effect liquid on her aunt that she couldn't swallow.

Katie's aunt finished her coffee and suddenly looked up at her. Aunt's eyes had softened as she studied Katie's face.

"Come here, child," Aunt said tenderly. Katie wasn't sure what she would do. She got up reluctantly and walked slowly over to her aunt. "Look at that hair." Aunt reached up and gently ran her fingers through Katie's hair. "When was the last time you washed it? I bet if you washed and brushed it, your hair would glow like your mother's used to. Come over to the sink. I'll wash it for you." Katie was glad to be able to walk away because she could feel the tears welling up ready to spill out. She was still afraid for her aunt to see them.

All day long her aunt surprised her by saying little things about her mother. She never mentioned chopping the wood. Instead, her aunt washed her hair, brushed it and fastened it back with a satin ribbon that she had found in a box beside her bed. Later they made bread and washed clothes together.

12

Aunt Clara Explains

The next morning, Katie again rose early and prepared the breakfast. She again put one small, white pebble into her aunt's coffee. Her aunt became even kinder to her than the day before.

"Katie, I've been going through that little sack of clothes you brought. You only have a couple of really good dresses. Goodness, they must have packed you up in such a hurry that they forgot to bring all of your thinks." She shook her head. "I know that your mother liked pretty things and I bet she spoiled you with them." She walked over to Katie and absently touched her hair. "You look so much like she did, you know? We were very close at one time. When she was little, I used to comb her long hair and fix her up real pretty. Everyone said that she was the beauty in the family, but I didn't care. I was just so proud of her. Maybe that's why she left here. Maybe we made too much of her. Anyway, I know she was a good person in her heart. I guess the way she raised you, she must have turned out okay, too." Katie looked up to see tears running down her face.

"Aunt Clara," she said as she put her arms around her aunt's thin waist and hugged her hard, "I think you turned out okay, too!"

"No, Katie, I'm an old, foolish woman. I have been very wicked and have taken a lot of anger out on you. I should be punished. What horrible things I said and did to you!" She put her head in her hands and sobbed so hard her shoulders shook. "I have behaved in such a mean way. I wasn't always like that. Can you ever forgive me?" She put her hand under Katie's chin and lifted her face up so Katie had to look right in her red, but somehow softer eyes.

"Aunt Clara, I just want you to be nice from now on. It doesn't matter about what happened before. Mommy told me that God always forgives us when we ask, so we must always forgive others, too." The tears were now running down Katie's face.

Aunt Clara pulled Katie to her and cried silently for a few minutes, then she pulled away and wiped her face.

"Well, child, we have to go to town to see about your clothes. You've grown some so maybe we will just buy you new ones. Then I can call that social worker and find out about the rest of your things." Aunt Clara sorted through the few things that Katie had brought with her.

"I'll be right back," Aunt Clara decided abruptly as she got up and went outside. She was back soon with Katie's bag of stuffed animals and other toys which she put on Katie's bed.

"I'm going to ask Larson to come up here and make you a shelf by your bed for these cute little creatures. I think maybe you need a little closet for your clothes too." Aunt Clara looked worried,

"Larson was my friend. I hope he can also forgive me. At any rate, we will find out tomorrow."

Katie sat very quietly. She wasn't sure how to take the sudden change in her aunt. She knew that she liked the nice aunt and that she was very grateful to Carp and to King Crab.

13

The Third Morning

On the third day, Katie again woke early and prepared the morning meal. She put the last pebble into her aunt's coffee. Her aunt woke and smiled at her.

"Look at you! Up so early and cooked the meal without being told. It smells delicious. I hate to say it, but you can cook better than me."

Katie's cheeks turned pink as she smiled. She felt warm and proud. "Good morning, Aunt."

"You don't have to call me Aunt. I loved it when you called me 'Aunt Clara' yesterday." She said as she came to the table with a big smile on her face. "It sounds like you know me and like me. That feels good!"

Aunt Clara's smile changed her from a drab-looking old lady into a warm, twinkling almost attractive person. Katie felt warm inside for the first time in months.

"I've been reading the cookbook that I found in the cupboard by the stove. I think it belonged to my grandmother. It tells me how to do everything," Katie decided to share the secret with her aunt.

Aunt Clara laughed a loud hoot and slapped her leg. "No wonder your cooking reminded me of Ma's. I never did have the patience to mess around with reading and trying new dishès. I was the one that was always working outside with Pa."

After they ate, Katie got up to wash the dishes. "No, you don't!" Her aunt jumped up. "You cooked so I need to wash the dishes, but first come over here. Let me brush your hair. Later, we are going to go to town and buy you some clothes like I said. You've earned them. Then I want to have you meet my friend, Larson's grandson, Mike. He's a nice boy. That way you will have a friend when you go to school next fall."

"Go to school next fall! Oh, Aunt Clara! But I thought you said I couldn't go to school because it is so far away."

"Oh, nonsense! Don't worry about what I said. I didn't tell you did I? This is only my summer place. Although sometimes I stay up here into the winter months if it is mild weather out. I have a little house down in town. You can walk to school from there. It's only a block away."

"I don't know what to say, Aunt Clara," Katie forgot herself and flung into her aunt's arms, "Thank you Aunt Clara!" She looked in her aunt's eyes, not certain is she should ask, but it had been troubling her for a long time. "Aunt Clara, can I ask you something else?"

Aunt Clara was looking at her intently, "Sure, Katie, what is it?"

"Is it--is it okay if we, can we go to church next Sunday?" You see, Katie hurried on afraid she had said too much, "Mommy and Daddy took me to church every Sunday and I miss it so much!"

Her aunt looked surprised, "You don't say! Well, I might shock a few righteous town people, but I don't see why not."

"Oh, thank you Aunt Clara, that makes me so happy!" She beamed at her aunt, "And Aunt Clara, I have just one more favor. Can I get the water, please?" Katie asked.

Her aunt hugged her, "Oh, you are a strange child, you are. You don't have to do that anymore. I don't know what go into me. I turned into a bitter, mean old lady, but no matter how wicked I was to you, you always returned it with gentleness. You never complained about the lot I gave you. Goodness knows, even the animals love you."

Aunt Clara got a far away look in her eyes, "I was taking all of my anger toward your mother out on you. You might wonder how I went from adoring your mother to hating her. I'm not really sure how it happened. I always had to do all work and your mother got to go off to school. She met your father and never came home. It broke Ma and Pa's hearts" Aunt Clara shook her head, as if to clear the memory from it.

She went on, "She just never came home until after they died. She said she always meant to, but there was always a reason she didn't have time. She blamed me for their death, but I think she was also mad at herself for not coming to see them before." The older lady took a deep breath, "You see they died in a fire. There used to be a large, beautiful log cabin here. Nothing like this old thing. But it burn to the ground. We didn't have insurance so this was the best I could replace it with."

Aunt Clara reached up to wipe the wettness from her face with her large, rough hand. "I never talked about this to no one before. They were sick, my ma and pa and not getting around well. I wrote your Ma but she never replyed back. I don't even know if it was the right address. Anyway, I was cooking and then I ran out of water so I went down to the creek to get some more. I don't know what happen when I was gone. I had left the food cooking on the stove, but the fire wasn't that hot. I just don't know. At any rate, when I got back the place was on fire. It took off so fast I couldn't even get inside. I tried to get in over and over again but the fire and smoke dove me back. It was horrible!" Aunt broke down crying, her shoulders shuddering.

Katie tried to comfort her, "It wasn't your fault Aunt Clara, you did everything you could to save them."

Aunt Clara breathed deeply and signed again, "That's not what your mother thought. The Red Cross found out where she was living, cause she had moved. Anyway, she and your father came to the funeral. They didn't have much to say to me and I never told them much. I think your mother blamed me."

"Did she say so?" Katie interjected.

"No, no, not in so many words, but I felt it."

"I think you are wrong!" Katie said softly, "I think you were both just too full of sadness, and you both thought the other one was mad, cause my Mommy was not mean, I think she loved you a lot. I always knew there was a sad side to her, now I know what it was."

"Maybe you are right. I know you are very wise for such a young thing," Aunt Clara blew her nose on an over-sized, cotton handkerchief, "I would like to think that she still loved me. I am so sorry I wasn't nicer to you when you first lost her. I will try to make it up to you."

"That's okay, it over now. I never knew about your mother and father. Mama never told me. It must have made her too sad." Katie almost whispered the last part. It hurt her to know that her mother had lost so much, too.

"Well it all happened before you were born. I'm not surprised that she didn't tell you. I guess you and I have something in common. We both lost parents that we loved dearly. Instead of being spiteful to you, I should have understood you more than anyone else. I did resent not having a chance to go to school and all the hard work I had to do, but I did love your grandparents more than life itself. In fact, when they died, it took a good deal of life out of me."

Aunt Clara stood up and ran her fingers through her hair. She glanced in the mirror, "My goodness! What a mess I am! I had better do something with my hair before we go to town."

"Aunt Clara, I really want to go get water at the creek. Can I go while you get ready? It won't take me long." She looked pleadingly at her aunt, "Please can I?"

Her aunt laughted out loud for the first time since Katie had met her. "Yes, of course, but don't stay long. Remember we have a date to get you some clothes. Her aunt began clearing the table.

Katie grabbed the water pail and ran past the squirrel who dashed out of her way, wondering why she didn't have any morsel for him to nibble on this morning. She didn't stop to talk to the birds or chipmunks. She ran down the path to the creek and leaped on her moss-covered rock. She lay down and looked into the water searching. "Carp! Carp!" she called, "Please come, I need to talk to you!"

The large fish didn't disappoint her. It swam slowly up to her and then in circles around her head. "It worked, Carp! It worked! I found the jar in my pocket and then I put the stones in my aunt's coffee. And it worked! She is nice now! Aunt Clara is really nice. She even looks like my Mama when she smiles. It changes her face just like the pebbles changed her heart."

Katie was brusting with happiness, "Oh thank you, Carp! I don't know what would have happened to me without you." He stopped swimming for a moment and looked up at her. Katie thought he winked and then he turned and swam away. It was the last time she would see him for a very long time.

Katie turned and raced back up the path toward her home in the beautiful woods and to her dear Aunt Clara. Her mind was full of the wonderful things she would be doing. She could hardly believe that she would be meeting the boy named Mike that lived only a short distance away. She wondered what he would be like. She sensed that he would become important to her, maybe even her best friend.

14

Best Friends

When Katie emerged from the pathway in the woods, she saw Aunt Clara walking towad the old station wagon. "Come on girl. Let's go to town!" She was smiling ear to ear.

It was the first time that Katie had left the little cabin in the woods since the tearful, frightening day she had arrived more than two months ago. She could barely contain herself as she jumped into the front seat next to Aunt Clara. She looked out the window eager to learn about her home town. The last time it was stormy and she couldn't see beyond the rain.

Katie was so excited to meet her new friend. She knew she would like him. Katie missed her old friends so much, but now she at least cound meet someone new. She was nervous and afraid to ask too many questions. They drove down the crooked, rutted trail from the cabin until the big oaks and maples thinned out and were replaced by a mixed variety of pine trees. Finally, they came to a wide dirt road which they drove on for a few more miles. They turned a corner and came to another little road.

Aunt Clara turned onto this road. "We are going to visit Larson first. His grandson is visiting him for the summer. Actually, he just lives in town a few miles away, but his ma works the split-shift a the dinner, so it is just easier if he stays here until her days off. His pa got killed in the Desert Storm War. She has to work and she doesn't want him to stay by himself" She pulled into a little, grassy drive way with two tracks running down the sides.

"Here we are," she said as they drove up to a big log cabin that was similar to her aunt's cabin only in that it was made of logs. It was huge and it was beautiful. The enormous porch ran all the way around the house with rocking chairs and swings scattered here and there. A big man in a red-checked shirt and jeans came out on the porch. His hair was pitch black and dark friendly eyes looked out of a rugged good looking face.

"Well, well, well! Look who decided to pay a visit. Howdy, Clara. You are the last person I expected to see out here. But what a nice surprise. I thought maybe you was still sore at me about what I said bout you being too mean to raise a kid." He laughed a warm booming laugh and ran down to meet them.

"Well, I decided that you knew what you were talking about," Clara smiled back, her eyes beaming at Larson. "This is my niece, Katie. The one we was talking about."

"Nice to meet you, Katie. Boy! Do you look like your ma. Oh, I'm sorry, I didn't mean to say anything that would make you sad."

"It's okay, Mr. Larson, I like looking like Mama. She was really pretty." Katie put her hand out to shake his big, callused warm hand.

"That she was. My name isn't Mr. Larson, Larson is just my first name, so you can just call me Larson, okay? By the way, I think your aunt Clara is kinda pretty too, don't you? I mean behind that sour look she always wears." He winked at Katie.

"Larson, behave yourself. Katie here has taught me a few lessons. The first one was to take a look at myself real good. Not just a glance in the mirror, but real good look right into my heart. I didn't like what I saw. I didn't like that sour look either so I got rid of it!" She said this with a big grin that made her eye twinkle. "In fact, if you don't mind, we would like to go to church with you this Sunday."

Larson just shook his head in disbelief, "Well who would have thought!" He turned to Katie. "You must be quite the miracle worker. I've been trying to get Chara to see the beauty that she buried years ago, for a long, long time. But she wouldn't listen to me. You come round for just a couple of months and presto the anger and bitterness melted away!" The whole time he was talking he was looking into Clara's eyes. Clara just looked back smiling at him.

"Come on in the house and meet Mike," he said to Katie. "He's in his room reading right now." They entered the cabin, which had a large stairway leading to the second floor. Everything was large even the furniture. Most of it was made out of logs and pine wood. Larson saw her looking around. "I made most of this stuff myself. That's what I do. I make wooden furniture. People come from all over the state to buy it, so it keeps me busy. I haul it into town to a little shop there."

"Hey, Grandpa! Who's here?" A boy about her age came tearing down the stairs. He had thick, black hair like his grandpa. He looked like a younger version of Larson, except he had the bluest eyes that Katie had ever seen.

"Whoa, there boy! Where's your manners? This is Katie, Clara's niece. They came to visit."

"Sorry, Grandpa, but nobody ever comes here to visit." He looked at Katie and smiled, "Hi Katie!"

Katie looked into his deep, deep blue eyes. Eyes that seemed familiar to her. It seemed to her that she knew Mike from somewhere. She smiled at him.

"Hi Mike!"

"Hey Katie, are you sure we didn't meet before? I mean I know you don't go to my school 'cause I know everybody there, but are you famous or something? Maybe I saw you on TV."

Katie laughed, "No, I'm not famous, but I know what you mean. It feels like I already know you, like we are already friends."

"Yeah, that's what I mean. Hey, do you want to go down by the river with me? That's my favorite place."

"Hey! Mine too!" For the first time since Katie had been driven to this county place in the North, she felt relaxed and totally at home. She was very comfortable with Mike. Now she was sure she had been right. They would be best friends. She knew she could tell him anything and she wanted to tell him everything.

"Mike," Katie said, "your grandpa has a funny first name. I thought it was his last name."

"I know," he said as they walked down the path to the river. "Look over there. See that rock? It's the best place to sit and read. Do you like to read? Oh, about my grandpa's name. His folks were Indian and the white people couldn't pronounce their last name so they just gave them names of things. My grandpa's great grandfather had a different name. Anyway, my grandpa's dad had a good friend with the last name of Larson so he named his son, my grandpa after him."

"That's interesting. It must have made them mad, though, that no one could say their name."

"No, I don't think so. Anyway, we still keep that name. It's Kitchigamig. It is also the name of an old tribe."

"What a neat name, but what was the last name your family was given?" she asked as she stirred a stick in the water.

"Carp," he said as he leaped onto his big, flat rock. "My name is Michael Carp."

Printed and bound by PG in the USA

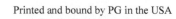

USA2019PG1L